Are You Blue Dog's Friend?

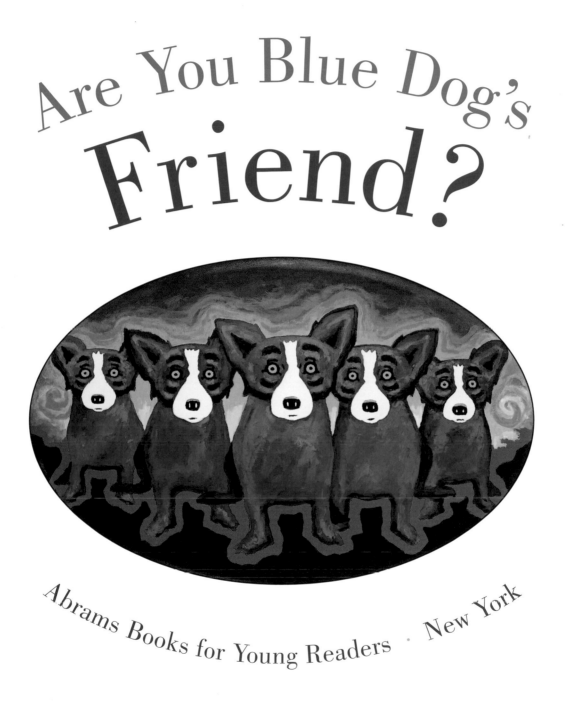

Abrams Books for Young Readers · New York

All of the artwork featured in this book
is oil or acrylic paint on canvas by
George Rodrigue.

Library of Congress Cataloging-in-Publication Data

Rodrigue, George.
Are you blue dog's friend? / by George Rodrigue.
p. cm.
ISBN 978-0-8109-4069-7 (Harry N. Abrams)
1. Color in art. 2. Tiffany (Dog) I. Title.

ND1490.R64 2009
[E]—dc22
2008047599

Text and illustrations copyright © 2009 George Rodrigue
Book design by Maria T. Middleton

Printed and bound in China
10 9 8 7 6 5 4 3 2 1

Abrams Books for Young Readers are available at special discounts when
purchased in quantity for premiums and promotions as well as fundraising
or educational use. Special editions can also be created to specification. For
details, contact specialmarkets@hnabooks.com or the address below.

HNA
harry n. abrams, inc.
a subsidiary of La Martinière Groupe

115 West 18th Street
New York, NY 10011
www.hnabooks.com

Hello.

My name is George and I am an artist.

This is me as a young boy.

This is Blue Dog.

He's one of my favorite subjects to paint.

I also like to paint things that are important to me,

like the people of my hometown,

New Iberia, Louisiana.

But my favorite things to paint . . .

Are Blue Dog's friends
loyal

Yes!

Everyone knows
that dogs are loyal,
but so are
Clarence,

Clotile, & Camille the Cats.

fuNn

Are Blue Dog's friends

Yes!

monkey business

He often gets into

with Maurice.

Are Blue Dog's friends

mUSICaL?

Yes!

He's a

HOUND DOG

with Elvis.

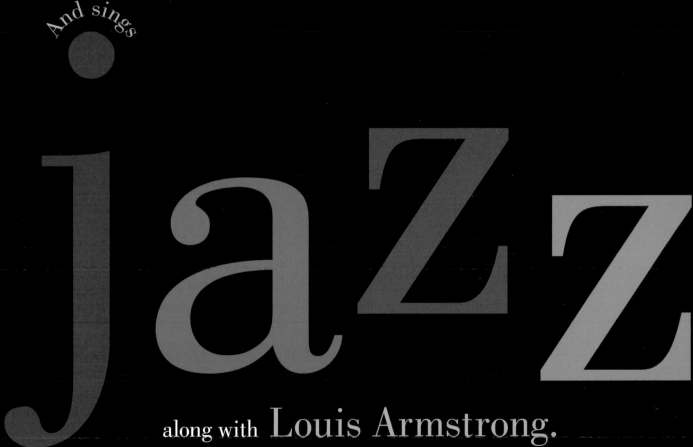

And sings

jaZz

along with Louis Armstrong.

Are Blue Dog's friends

OUT OF
THIS
WORLD?

Yes!

When Blue Dog visits

his friends in

s p a c e ,

he dresses as

an astronaut.

Are
Blue Dog's
friends

tr**1**ckster**s**?

Yes!

During
Mardi
Gras,
Blue Dog and his friends
dress up like

Are
Blue
Dog's
friends
always
with
him?

It sometimes seems that way.

But I often paint Blue Dog by himself.

Is Blue Dog lonely without his friends?

IS BLUE DOG
BLUE?

Blue Dog
is never lonely,
because he's with . . .

You!